A
BABY
CRIES

A SHORT STORY

RYNE GREEN

ISBN-13: 978-0-9982190-2-8

DEDICATION

To Matt Damon, a terrific actor, a better friend

A BABY CRIES

Clyde Blevins remembers the pride he felt when he cut the umbilical cord, the love he felt when he held his baby daughter Mary in his arms for the first time. While she was sucking on her fingers, he looked at his tired wife, Maria, who smiled at him. He thought of all of the precious moments that the three of them would share together. Their first Christmas and birthdays together, the first time she would walk towards him, when she'd say her first words. He knew that when they got home, life would never would be the same again.

Those treasured memories that he was so excited for would never happen. Of the four months they had together, his few memories of Mary outside of feeding and changing her were those times when she cried, and he felt a fatherly instinct to take her in his arms to soothe her. He couldn't stand hearing his baby crying, whether she was in pain or discomfort. Maria said that he would probably end up babying her for the rest of her life. And she was right.

Now, he wondered, if he had known what would happen, would he even have tried to have a child in the first place? Would he have surrendered the pride and joy of it all if it meant no longer feeling the pain of loss? It was an easy question for those who had not experienced it, but a much harder one when you had. To love someone unconditionally meant risking unimaginable loss, one that you could never possibly prepare for.

Mary was just four months old when she went to sleep and never woke up. She would never get to experience all of life's wonders and woes. Clyde wondered if there was anything he could have done if he had noticed it earlier. With those thoughts came fear. A fear that suggested that his daughter's death was on his hands. He remembered how she looked so peaceful in her crib, a baby doll at her side. He brushed her blonde hair with his hand. The moment he touched her head, everything changed.

At first, a true and primal dread crept through Clyde and Maria as they desperately tried to wake their baby girl from her eternal sleep. When Clyde got no response from the baby he held in his quivering arms, he felt as if someone drove a shovel through him, digging every good part of him away. He did not cry. Or if he did, he was far too numb to feel it.

The paramedic and coroner were there in a matter of minutes. Judging by their calm handling of the situation, Clyde knew this wasn't their first time. He didn't pay attention to his neighbors standing by their house, watching what was unfolding. They were probably still trying to figure out what happened, but didn't have to courage to walk up to them.

He didn't really care who was watching, anyway. He just sat next to his wife and mourned with her, holding their child's life body in their arms. The coroner allowed them one last moment with their baby. One of the personnel tried to comfort them, telling them that these things just happen. She was an older woman with greying hair, probably around his own mother's age.

Since the moment of realization set in, he and his wife were in a state of wild mourning. Their home was their place of mourning. But when the cops came, that all changed. When they arrived, they instructed Clyde and Maria to leave their home. As the officers walked him outside, he began to realize that they were doing an investigation. A cop asked Maria if they could talk in the back lawn, to which she could barely nod. Clyde was going to follow, but one of the officers grabbed him by the shoulder and told him they were going to the porch. As they walked outside, he noticed that some of the officers were looking around their house and could hear cabinet doors shutting from the kitchen. He wondered just what it was that they were looking for.

The cops had some questions for him. He didn't understand what was left to ask until it hit him like a truck: the police were investigating potential murder. He was separated from his wife because they were interrogating them. The cops inside were looking through the house in search of any incriminating evidence. Moments earlier, they were balling their eyes out. He saw the redness in his wife's eyes. Now, they were suspected of murdering the love of their lives.

The questions themselves weren't that hard to answer, yet the thought that they were even asked was devastating. His daughter's toothless smile flashed in his head. How could he have ever hurt something so precious to him?

He soon reunited with his wife, but their baby was gone. The officer told them that the coroner had to take her to confirm the cause of death. Clyde had desperately wanted to hold his baby one more time. He made the grave mistake of asking how they could confirm the cause of death. Their answer felt like a knife diving into his own heart: an autopsy. The next time he saw her, she had huge gashes on her. The image burned into his memory.

"There's nothing you could have done to stop this." "These things just happen without reason." The professionals all echoed these sentiments in an attempt to console him and Maria. But it did not make him feel better. It did not make him feel better when the police officers suspected foul play. It did not make him feel better when the doctors cut open their baby girl. How could it make anyone feel better?

After the funeral for their daughter, the house felt so quiet, so empty. The principal told Clyde to take as much time as he needed, but he still came up with some assignments for his science class to work on while he was in grieving. Maria could only get a week away from the bank. He supposed the banks were more indifferent to their employees' mental states than a school. However, that week they spent felt torturous to him.

They had plenty of time to themselves and nothing to do with it. They only thought about Mary, something that was too painful to do. They were both in shock and they both felt responsible. The guilt they were burdened with was unbearable to them. Clyde tried to distract himself by going on the internet and looking up anything to keep his mind busy. Maria went to the living room and played the piano that she'd had since she was 12, always collapsing in tears.

They also had to deal with calls from those claiming that they haven't paid their bills yet. The officers and doctors warned them about those who would try to take advantage of those in mourning. It seemed that a new, uglier side of humanity showed itself once you lost a child.

Clyde didn't eat or sleep. He just walked around the house in his bathrobe, visiting each room like he did when comforting Mary. The one room he stayed out of was Mary's. The crib that she slept in that day was still there, along with her favorite doll. It wasn't just the crib, though. Everything that reminded them of Mary went into that room: Bottles, baby plates, toys, the car seat. Out of sight, out of mind, or so they say.

Although it had only been four months, he had become accustomed to parenthood. Waking up at odd hours of the night to crying, spending hard-earned money on diapers and baby food, bathing the baby in the sink, cleaning up their messes and staying home when they were sick were all part of their normal lives as parents.

Now those responsibilities were gone and they desperately wanted them back, so very much. Now they had no responsibilities, and they realized something they wished they never had: how easy life could be without a child. They had more time for themselves and more money, with nothing to do with either. This new convenience only fueled Clyde's guilt over Mary. It felt like he was being rewarding for going through such a horrible thing.

Clyde and Maria's conversations were small talk at best. "Did you sleep well?" "How was your day?" They didn't spend dinner together. Instead, each night saw a cup of instant ramen for Clyde and a grilled cheese sandwich for Maria.

Clyde knew they were trying to avoid thinking

about their daughter, and he felt disgusted by it. Was it okay for them to act like this? Pretend that nothing happened? That she never existed? Was this what life was going to be for now on? He couldn't find an answer to these questions, so he continued to distract himself with little things.

He slept on the couch since the bed felt empty without their daughter lying in between them. He had dreams of being in a forest. He heard his daughter crying somewhere in the distance, and he would search for her. The forest was thick with trees and bushes, but they did little to stop him. He would be reunited with his daughter. When he got close to her, his alarm was a constant reminder of cruel reality.

By the end of the week, Clyde was grateful to go back to work.

Four months had passed since Mary's death. Four months had passed, and he hadn't felt much of anything. He got out of bed. After the first week, it became easier to return to the bed. He looked at Maria's side and saw that she was already up. He went into the bathroom to a fogged mirror and wet floor. As the shower rained down on him, he stood motionlessly for a moment before cleaning himself.

Once he got changed for work, he headed to the kitchen where his wife had prepared him a cup of coffee. She leaned against the counter as she silently sipped her coffee. He reached out toward his cup until he realized what it said, in bold black lettering:

World #1 DAD!

He sure didn't feel like it.

"It was the only clean cup we had," Maria said. "I'm sorry." Her eyes told him that she instantly regretted not rinsing out a cup.

"No, it's okay." He grabbed the cup. He knew it wasn't intentional. With what they were going through, they sometimes forgot the smaller details. They both drank their coffee in silence. Four months back, one of them would drink coffee while the other fed Mary. Monday, Wednesday, Friday and every other Sunday were his shifts. Sometimes she would get upset and try to knock the spoon of mush away. There were days when she cried when she was forced to eat.

Perhaps the most noticeable change in their life now was that silence in the house. When nothing was on, it was as quiet as a graveyard. He would talk to Maria sometimes, but it usually sounded exactly like when they drank their coffee. Nothing. Absolutely nothing. Clyde missed the days when his mornings were filled with the sound of crying.

"Do you know what you want to have for dinner tonight?" Maria asked, flashing him a smile. It'd been awhile since he saw her smile, and he almost forgot just how pretty it was.

"It doesn't matter to me," he said.

"No, really what do you want?" she pressed on, tired of these one-sided conversations, wanting him to open up more. To bring some normalcy back into their lives. He understood where she was coming from and appreciated the effort, but he wasn't ready.

"Just whatever you want." His glance told her not to push any further.

"Okay then." Her smile disappeared. She finished her coffee and placed it in the sink. "I got to get going. Don't be late for work."

"I know." But he wasn't sure if he would make it on time. Not that the principal minded if he was late.

He could probably miss first period entirely and the staff would give him a pass. She tried to kiss him before she left, but he wasn't in the mood for it and she just left.

Clyde finished his coffee in silence and glanced at his watch. It would be best if he headed to school. He made his way through the hallway, which meant passing Mary's room. Mary's picture was hanging from the door, below it was a cross and a quote from the Bible. He looked the other way. He walked past the room, but that was when he heard it.

"WAAAAAAHHH!" Clyde stopped dead in his tracks, the noise wailing behind him. He turned and saw nothing. His heart was in his throat now. What was that noise? He realized it was coming from Mary's room. He stood outside of the door, unsure of what to do.

"WAAAAAAHHH!" The noise continued. There was an urge in him to hurry into the room, but he wasn't sure why. There was something about the noise that was familiar to him.

"WWWAAAAAAAAAAHHHHHHHHH!" It was this third howl that he realized it was the sound of a baby crying. Was there...a baby in the room? No, he told himself, that's impossible. He tried to convince himself, but the crying was far too real for him to imagine it. It was too powerful to ignore. His trembling hand reached out and grabbed the doorknob. He held it for a pause before slowly turning the knob. He stopped and looked at the picture of his daughter. She was in her pink pajamas with hearts and stars pattern, that beautiful toothless grin spread across her face. It brought back painful memories fresh as an open wound.

"What am I doing?" He pulled himself from the

door. He needed to get out of the house. He needed to get to work. As he made his way to the door, the crying was ringing throughout the house, much louder than before. Something urged him to go back to the room. He forced himself toward the door, telling himself that he was just hearing things as he took his first step outside. Once the door was slammed shut, the crying stopped. He let out a deep sigh of relief and leaned back on the door. It was quiet now, something he didn't expect to feel relief from. His hand found its way to his forehead, surprised by how much sweat had formed in such a short time.

He realized that he would be late at this rate. Suddenly, he really did want to make it on time. He hurried to his car and started pulling out, but not before taking one last look at the house. He wondered if he was losing his mind.

"Everyone settle down now," Clyde said as he finished taking roll. The room started to quiet down at his demand. In his experience, middle school students were at their rowdiest during first period and last period. But the kids had been more compliant these days, and it wasn't hard for him to figure out why. He sat down behind his desk and began calling out names.

"Is that everyone?" One of the students raised his hand.

"You forgot about me, sir," the young man said.

"Sorry about that, Brad," he said. He wasn't fully there. He was thinking about what had happened at the house. Before he was married, he couldn't stand the sound of a crying baby. He found babies annoying and wished the parents would shut them up. Now he still couldn't stand it, but for entirely different reasons. The sound of crying was almost maddening to him.

"Sir, who's going to give the animal fact today?" One of the students raised her hand. This bought him back to reality. He needed to get to work.

"Right, uh, today it's Casey's turn. What do you have for us?" Before he started with his lessons, he had a student give a fact about any kind of animal they found interesting. It was a good way for them to get points and be involved with class.

A student with blonde hair that sat in the front stood up. Of all of the students in his morning class, she was the shortest. She could've passed herself as an elementary schooler and no one would notice. She felt around in her backpack and pulled out a piece of paper. "My animal fact for the day is about the Cuckoo bird."

"Wait, those things actually exist?" one of the kids in the back interrupted. "I thought those were just toy birds on old clocks." He started to loudly mimic the bird call, or at least what he thought they sounded like, and the class laughed.

"Settle down everyone." The rowdiness died down at his command. "Casey, please continue."

"Thank you, Mr. Blevins." She smiled, looked at her paper and cleared her throat. "There are several species of Cuckoo birds, and what I found interesting is that some of these species are brood parasites."

"Really? Tell us what that is?" He too would be invested in these facts, especially when it was something he had never heard of.

"Well, based on what I've read, brood parasites are creatures that have others raise their young." This caught the attention of many of the class. "There are several ways of doing this, but the cuckoo birds search for nests that have eggs. Once they find one, they knock the eggs out of the nest." Some of the girls gasped at this. "The mother cuckoo bird then lays its eggs there. When it is done, they fly away and have the nest's owner raise their chicks for them."

"That's very interesting," he said. During the weeks after Mary's passing, animal facts were an effective way to get his mind off of everything. "Are there questions any of you have?" The boy who interrupted her raised his hand. His name was Darryl, and he was something of a class clown. "Yes, Darryl?"

"So, if the eggs hatch, won't the bird know that it wasn't their eggs? Won't it just fly away?"

"That's a very good question. Do you know why that is, Casey?"

"Well, I wondered that too," she explained. "It turns out that many birds are actually pretty dumb." The class chuckled. "Since it's in their nest and crying for food, they assume that it is their own. But if the bird does abandon the nest, the parent cuckoo finds the bird and thrashes its new nest and even forces it to take care of the chick."

"Wow, cuckoo birds are dicks," one of the students in the back said. The class burst out in laughter at this. Clyde himself couldn't help but agree with the statement.

"But that's so sad," said Betty, the girl sitting next to Casey.

"What is?" Casey asked.

"The cuckoo bird kills the other bird's babies," she said. "The bird that knows that the chick isn't theirs must know their own chicks were killed. They must be so sad."

"Yeah," Clyde said, now feeling empathy for

the bird. "That is pretty sad, isn't it?" Betty's expression changed to that of a realization. She had unintentionally opened some wound. But it wasn't just her now; the rest of the class was uncomfortably silent. The air would've felt more fitting at a funeral than a classroom.

"I'm so sorry," Betty squeaked out, looking away from him.

"No, no, it's okay everyone." He attempted to cheer up the class. "Thank you for the new fact, Casey, that was very interesting."

"Thank you, sir." The way she said it sounded like a child being scolded by a passive-aggressive parent. He wondered if she may have regretted choosing that fact now.

The mood remained unchanged as he looked around the class. He supposed this was something that happened even after months had passed. Weeks after the death, it became clear that once you lose a child, it became a part of your identity. And it changed how people behaved around you.

Before the death, their neighbor and friends would ask if they planned on having a second child, to which they answered they did. After all, they didn't want Mary to be alone when they were gone. But after the death, no one dared asked the question again. Their friends were very careful about what they said around them. Many avoided complaining about their children when talking to them. He supposed it would be like someone complaining about a leak in their attic to a homeless man. But it didn't help. It merely served as a reminder of his late baby.

That was another change to his reality: everything became a reminder. The baby formula that was in their cabinet still. The children's channels that he would flip through on the television. Every commercial about life insurance, every show featuring a child, every time a baby cried, every time he walked by her room. Even the house itself. Everything reminded him of Mary.

"Well, it's time to begin today's lesson," he said, standing up and walking toward the chalkboard. "Everyone please open your book to page 178." He heard the shuffling of pages and creaking of desk chairs. He began to wish their rowdiness would return as they began their session.

Clyde pulled into his driveway and parked outside the garage. Since his wife had the expensive, newer car, it got garage privileges. The rest of the school day went much better for him, but the memory of his first class was the definitive moment of the day. He looked through the car's tinted window at the house and thought what would happen when he stepped inside. Would he hear that crying again? If he was just hearing things this morning, that would be cause enough for concern, but if he heard it again, he may just have to leave the house.

His wife was already home, most likely giving piano lessons to the neighbor's kid. She worked at the bank, but took up a side gig as a tutor. Originally, it was for the extra money to spend on Mary, but she continued to do it. Perhaps it was because of a sense of duty, or maybe she liked having a child in the house again. It's not like they were in the need for more money.

He wondered if Maria heard the crying as well. Maybe she was hearing the crying right now. With his lunchbox in hand, he got out of the car and walked along the pavement to his porch. The cold February air sent chills through him as he wrapped his arms around himself. The weather channel said there was a very good chance of snow coming through. Lord knows it was cold enough. He walked up the small flight of stairs to his porch and stood at the door. He knew someone was playing the piano, and judging by the amateurish sound and the mishaps, he assumed it must have been a student playing. That meant she didn't hear the crying. Had she heard something, she would have sent the kid home.

As he reached out toward the knob, he noticed that his hand was trembling slightly. He must have been more nervous than he thought. He took a deep breath and turned the knob. The door slowly opened, and the sound of the piano became clear as it leaked out. He heard no crying as he stepped through. He felt a wave of relief as he closed the door behind him. He took his jacket off and put it up on the rack. He walked to the living room where the piano was. He saw his wife at the piano and next to her was one of the neighbor boys, whose name he forgot.

She looked at him and smiled softly before swiftly putting her focus back on the boy. "Very good, Jacob. I think you are getting better." He knew she was lying, but she always believed positive reinforcement and encouragement was the best approach to improving.

"You really think so?" the boy asked with a big grin. The boy couldn't have been older than 10 years old. You got to start them when they are young, he guessed.

"Of course." She smiled at him and looked

back at Clyde. "Honey, could you fix us a bag meal? We're almost done."

He nodded and walked toward the kitchen. As he walked away, the music resumed. He opened the deep freezer door. Cold air enveloped him as he looked for something to cook. Bag meals were simple enough to cook. He saw one that had chicken in it and decided on it. He grabbed the partly frozen bag and shut the door. Now he just needed a pot.

He didn't remember which cabinet they kept the pots in, so he just started opening them at random. It wasn't until his third try that he found what he was looking for. He lifted the black, steel pot out of the cabinet. When he got it out, he noticed that something was behind it. It was Mary's favorite bottle that had hearts on it. She would always flash that famous grin when she saw it. There were times when she refused other bottles full of formula for it. Before he could think too much on it, he slammed the cabinet door a little too hard. A loud smack raced across the house and the music stopped.

"What was that?" his concerned wife asked.

"Sorry, I shut the cabinet door too hard," he called to her. He grabbed the pot and placed it on the stove.

"How did you do that?" she asked, not knowing the context.

"Sorry, my hand slipped. That's all." He turned on the stove and emptied the bag into the pot. As he waited for the stove to heat up, he could hear the piano again. He always thought that when Mary turned six years old, Maria would teach her to play the piano. He never understood why some parents had their children go to special classes. He knew this one couple who took their two-year-old daughter to dancing class. He wasn't a fan. He thought that kids should just be kids while they had the chance.

"WAAAAAAHHHHHHH!"

"What?" Clyde heart skipped a beat when he heard that familiar sound. "No."

"WAAAAAAAAAAHHHHHHHH!" The almost hypnotic sound shot through the house once more, mixing with the sound of the piano.

"Not again. Not again." He started to panic. The kind of panic that calls for action. Like that of a mother bear protecting her cub. But he didn't know what to do, and it only got louder. He thought he might have just been hearing things in the morning, but this felt too real to be his imagination. This had to be real!

"WAAAAAAAAAAAAHHHHHHHH!" He had to get Maria. She must be hearing this, too. Ignoring the pot full of food, he left the kitchen and hurried to the living room with the crying accompanying him each step of the way. His heartbeat felt like a shotgun going off, and his pulse felt like he was running for his life. He began to remember who that cry belonged to. As he got closer to the living room, he heard the piano playing. *"How in the hell are they still playing the piano?"* he asked himself.

He made it to the living room and couldn't believe that his wife was just sitting there as the crying got louder. Was the piano louder than the crying? No, that's impossible, he thought. Maria lifted her head from the piano keys and looked at him.

"Is something wrong?" She smiled innocently at him. She signaled to the kid to keep playing.

"What's wrong?! Don't you hear that?" He raised his hand for her to stay quiet.

"WWAAAAAHHHHHH!" The crying was much louder than before. There's no way she couldn't hear it! She still had the same puzzled look on her face.

"Don't you hear that?" he asked. He was breathing heavily as the sweat rolled down the face, less out of panic and more out of concern that he may, indeed, be crazy.

"Hear what?" she asked.

"Hear what?" he scoffed. "YOU DON'T HEAR THAT?" The crying continued and she just sat there. The boy next to her had an uncomfortable expression, like a child sitting in the back seat of the car as his parents argue. A mixture of discomfort, fear, uncertainty and anxiety. He just sat there, pushing down on the piano keys.

"Honey, are you okay? You don't look well." Her smile had now turned into something else, not completely discernible. "I don't hear anything." At this point, he started feeling angry and agitated. In part with his wife's deafness to the crying and in part with the boy playing the piano. He wasn't even playing anything now, just mashing his fingers against random keys.

He marched up to the piano. "Well maybe you will if he stopped playing this for a FEW DAMN SECONDS!" He slammed his fist on the piano. The boy jumped back and looked at him with terror. The boy looked away from him and quickly dropped his hands to his side. The music had stopped.

"CLYDE!" Maria snapped in disbelief and wrapped her arms around the boy as if to protect him. Maybe it was her motherly instincts kicking in. "WHAT HAS GOTTEN INTO YOU?"

"Shhh!" He put his finger to his mouth. "Just listen for a second. They waited, but there was nothing now. No crying, no piano music, not even the buzzing of flies. Just three silent people waiting to hear something.

"What are we listening for?" Maria asked, about at the end of her wits. Rage was in her eyes. He could tell that she was holding herself back from shouting at him in the presence of a child. Even at their worst moments in front of Mary, she would never shout at him, and she expected the same of him.

"But I…I heard it. It was as clear as day to me. I thought that if he stopped…you would hear, too." He could only imagine what she was thinking of. That look in her eye said that he was losing it.

"Jacob, why don't you head home for the day. Just give this back to your mom." She helped him up and handed him the 10-dollar bill.

"Okay. Thank you." He tried to hide how upset he was, but Clyde could tell by his voice that he was shaken up. His eyes watered as he passed them. They waited until they heard the door shut.

"Maria, look I-"

"WHAT THE HELL HAS GOTTEN INTO YOU!" she shouted, her anger flowing out freely now. "How could you do that!?" She was starting to shake now, as she often did when she shouted.

"I-I heard it," he repeated. "It was real."

"Heard what?" She asked.

"It was a baby crying!" he shouted back, stunning her. Now anger was replaced with sympathy as if she understood what was going on now. "It wasn't just any baby either…it was Mary." Tears began to form in her eyes and she started to wipe them away.

"Clyde…Mary died," she mournfully said.

"I know, but I heard it. I know it sounds crazy,

but I heard it. And I heard it this morning, too." He put it all out there for her.

"Sweetie, you're just imagining-"

"I'M NOT THOUGH!" he shouted, completely certain about it. "You think I wouldn't recognize my own daughter's crying? It was REAL!"

"We're just in mourning," she tried to reason. "When my grandpa passed away, I thought I saw him in crowds. You're still grieving is all. I'm still grieving."

"Oh really?" he said. "Is teaching the kid how to play piano part of your grieving process?"

"Is there something wrong with me giving piano lessons?" Tears began rolling down her face.

"Well, I can't help but think you are just trying to replace her," he said. "You wanted to teach Mary the piano. Well, now you don't have to wait with the kid!"

She just stood there in disbelief. He didn't really mean it, but wanted to make her as upset as he was. "How dare you…" She threw up her arms in the air. "You know what? Just forgot about a bag meal, I'm going out to eat. Maybe you will have time to cool off." She walked by him and slammed the door on her way out.

"Fine, you do that!" he shouted even though she had already left. "I'm going to prove you wrong." He knew where the crying was coming from. He made his way down the hallway to reach his daughter's room. The photo of her toothless grin hung from the door. Pushing past his anxiety, he clutched the knob, twisted it open, and didn't take a second to step inside the room.

Everything was where it was supposed to be. All her toys were in the little toy box that his parents got for her. The baby plates were on the dressing drawers that stood in the corner of the room. In the top corner was a net hammock full of stuffed animals. He remembered buying several of those dolls, like the stuffed tiger that he got for her at the zoo. Dust covered much of everything: dust clogs were in the fur of the dolls, and dust blanketed the drawer and crib.

As he walked to the crib, his heart was beating harder now than before over what he might find in it. He glanced into it and was disappointed to find there was nothing. He was scared by what this meant. Was he really just hearing things? And if he was, why now? Had it happened the month after, that would be more reasonable. But four months after?

"No, no, that can't be," he reassured himself. "The crying was real." Of that he was certain. He thought about it and realized he needed to wait until the crying came back. He felt that if he waited until the crying started again, then he could find the source. He shouldn't have gone to his wife when the crying started. He should have come here.

He looked around the room and noticed something was amiss. It was the window that looked out on their backyard. It was halfway open. Did they forget to shut the window? He supposed it was possible. They hadn't been in the room for months. Due to the circumstances of their last visit, an open window would be an easy oversight. He shut it down.

He walked out the room and closed the door behind him. When Maria returned home, he would apologize for what he had said. He would wait in the living room until the crying started again. If the crying started when Maria was asleep, that would be better since he wouldn't risk her walking in on him.

Things didn't go exactly as Clyde hoped when Maria returned home. For the better part of an hour, she ignored him when he tried to get her attention. He supposed it was understandable since their fight was probably the most hurtful they'd had. But after some time, they did make up. He felt some guilt, knowing that he pushed some buttons about Mary. Guilt over things he'd said in the heat of the moment had a way of biting him in the ass.

It was shortly after midnight when he was lying in bed. Outside it was snowing quite a bit and had been since 10 that night. School was called off in advance and many assumed it would be for the rest of the week. His wife had already gone to sleep, but he was fully awake. Normally he would be the first to fall asleep whenever he felt a warm blanket, but not tonight. He was determined to stay awake until he heard that crying again. He would have to be careful not to wake Maria when he got out of bed. He didn't like the thought of explaining what he intended to do.

Light from the lamppost shined into the room so he could see fairly well despite the drapes they used. Before the lamppost was put up, the room was completely dark; he couldn't even see his hands. When it was put up, the light was maddening to him. They did whatever they could to block the light. Eventually they settled with partial success when their drapes blocked some of it. Since then, they had grown used to the partly lit room. Perhaps that's how all things are. Given enough time, slight annoyances become familiar, something you don't notice much anymore.

To his side was the glowing light of the alarm clock set to go off at 6:30 in the morning. Although their phones were louder alarms, having the clock next to him helped his blood to start flowing when he reached out for it.

He turned to look at his wife who was peacefully sleeping next to him. The side of her head was resting on her pillow. Without her makeup, she looked a tad older than she should with faint wrinkles starting to form. No doubt because of the stress and sorrow she had felt these past four months. She was still as beautiful as ever, but it was a new type of beauty. One that only those who've weathered through hardship could possess. He wondered if he had changed in some way as well, be it physically or mentally, and if those changes were good or bad.

Such thoughts began to wear on him as he waited for the cries. Despite his determination, his eyes began to feel heavy as he stared at his sleeping wife. He became weary and the thought of sleep became very appealing to him. His eyelids began to lower, and his attempts to resist were futile as his eyes shut closed.

"WWAAAAAAAAAAAHHHHHHHH!" His eyes immediately opened, his consciousness returned tenfold. He was impressed by his restraint in not jolting up, as he slowly eased himself out of the bed. He tiptoed to their bathroom to put his bathrobe on. Once that was done, he made his way through their room and to the hallway.

"WWAAAAAAAAAAAHHHHHHHH!" The crying continued as he slowly crept through the hallway. It felt much colder in the hallway than it did in his room, like stepping out in the snow. With each step against the cold wooden floor, chills shot up through him. His nervousness came back as he moved closer to Mary's room. The hallway felt like it was stretching out further and further, the room forever out of his reach.

His mind went blank as he approached the door. He only came back to when he felt the doorknob in his hand. The steel knob felt cold as his grip tightened. He turned it and opened the door, greeted by a wave of cold air.

Confusion surfaced as he stepped into the room, wondering why it was so cold. He wrapped his arms around himself. He was once again surprised by what he saw. The window was open. "*I shut that, didn't I?*" he thought as he walked toward the window. It must have been the reason why it was so cold in the hallway. He closed the window and it felt familiar to him, and he recalled shutting it. So how was it open now? Was someone trying to break in? He looked at the rim of the window and it still looked dusty. If someone came in through the window, then they would have unintentionally wiped some of the dust off. And besides that, there was no sign of someone breaking in.

He glanced through the window and already the ground was covered in at least two feet of snow with more on the way. It was then he noticed something in the snow-covered ground. He wasn't sure what they were, but there was a pattern of them in the snow. He tried to look closer, but couldn't see well in the dark. What he saw looked almost like tracks. But they weren't like any tracks he had seen before. He stood there wondering just what they were.

Just outside, he saw something in the dark woods, something shadowy hiding behind the trees. He couldn't get a good view and was about to call out to it. Suddenly, a bright blinding light.

"What?" he said, dazed and distorted. For a brief second, he couldn't see, but once it returned he saw nothing. "What? What?" He looked around the room and felt misplaced. This wasn't his room? Another question came to mind: What was he doing in the room again?

"WWWAAAAAAAAAAAAAAAAAAHHHHHH HHH!" He was snapped out of his thoughts when he heard the crying. "*That's right,*" he told himself, he didn't have time to think. He only came for one reason. He turned to the crib and although it was dark, he could tell that something was in there. Whatever it was, he could tell that it was reaching out for something. He just stood there in disbelief, thinking that what he was looking at was impossible.

His heart was beating in his throat as he walked to it. Although it was only a couple of steps to the crib, it felt like an hour passed with each step. Anxiety hit him with the force of a truck. He took a deep breath as he looked into the crib. When he saw it… it… it…it. He smiled a warm smile.

"Hey there, Mary," he said with delight. Mary looked up at him and gave him her famous toothless grin and reached out for him. "Are you having trouble going to sleep?" He reached into the crib and lifted her out. He carried her to the rocking chair in the corner and sat in it. He began rocking his baby back and forth, cradling the young girl in his arms. She felt so small. Her short mop of hair looked like golden thread and her blue eyes were vast oceans. It was hard to believe that she came from someone like him.

He knew that it wasn't possible, wasn't sure what was happening and knew she couldn't be real. And yet, as he looked at her, there was no doubt in his mind that it was her. Whether it was the ghost of his deceased daughter or an act of God, it was her. That's all that mattered to him. He didn't feel cold anymore.

In fact, he felt a wonderful warmth, a sense of harmony, a renewal of life. The days of mourning were over for him, his daughter was back. That was when a thought came to his mind.

"I bet you're hungry," he said and she smiled. Her giggle was like music to him. "Alright, let's go get something out of the cabinet." He got up and put her back in the crib. "I'll be back in just a second." When he put her in the crib, the coldness returned to him, but it was one that he knew would pass.

He left the room and headed toward the kitchen. He saw some formula when he was looking for a pot earlier that day. Once he was there, he opened up the cabinet that had the formula. Now he needed a bottle and he knew where to find one. He opened the cabinet door that concealed the pots and reached in. He felt the bottle in his hand and pulled it out. He could picture the smile on her face when she saw her favorite bottle.

"WWWAAAAAAAAAAAAAAAHHHHHHHHHHHH!" The crying sent a jolt of panic toward him. He recognized hunger and impatience.

"Hang on, sweetie. I'll be there soon," he whispered to himself as he filled the bottle up with the formula. When he was finished, he hurried as quickly as he could while avoiding waking his wife back in the room. When he got in, she was still crying for her daddy. "It's okay. I got what you wanted."

He lifted Mary out of the crib and sat down in the chair. "Here you go." He lowered the bottle down to her and she started sucking the formula. As she drank, she looked at him. He just looked back with a smile. He knew there was a reason that only he could hear her. But what was it?

Could it have been that he could hear her because Maria had moved on, perhaps even forgetting her daughter and now she is being punished for it? He told himself that wasn't true. She loved Mary as much as he did, if not more. She carried her inside for over nine months and endured pain he couldn't imagine.

Yet he couldn't think of a better answer. Maybe it wasn't intentional on her part, just not noticing it happen as she was forced to keep up with the world. He pitied her if that turned out to be the case. As he rocked in the chair, he thought he felt a pinch on the nape of his neck.

"What?" He turned and saw nothing but the wall. His attention to Mary returned when she burped and started giggling. With a giggle of his own, he started patting her on the back to see if she needed to burp again. She looked tired as she began to yawn. It was time for her to go to bed.

He placed her back in the crib. He looked to the net of stuffed dolls and grabbed the tiger that he got her at the zoo. He put it beside her and she curled up against it and fell asleep. He stood over her and just smiled. He hadn't felt this happy in such a long time.

Perhaps it was that happiness that made him so exhausted. It was time for him to go back to bed. He stepped out of the room and closed the door gently so not to wake Mary. He made his way back into his room and got into bed. His wife was deep in sleep and wasn't disturbed at all. He closed his eyes and felt like he could finally have a good night's sleep.

It had been a week since Maria and Clyde had their fight. Their yard was covered in five feet of snow and school had been out. Maria had some regrets of not pursuing a career in teaching if just for the days off of work she could have. Not to mention it would be easier to plan vacations with her husband: a summer break was much simpler than asking for time off at the bank. She liked to imagine herself as a teacher, carpooling with her husband, gossiping with the other teachers, and being able to understand each other's complaints after a hard day. And on snow days they could have slept in. She always imagined how nice that must be. Having a day off and still getting paid.

Clyde seemed to be happy about the week. At first, she was relieved to hear this. He hadn't been eager to have time off since that week after Mary's death. She thought that this newfound excitement meant that he was turning back to normal.

But now, there was something about her husband that was off. He would wake up when she did and take a shower. On most snow days, he would just sleep in until around 9. It was like he had something to do, something that couldn't wait a couple of hours. At night when she'd wake up early, she noticed that her husband wasn't in bed. At first, she thought that he just went to the bathroom and thought nothing of it, but it had become consistent each night.

She noticed the baby formula wasn't in the cabinet anymore. She had meant to get rid of it, but would get distracted and forget about it. Could he have gotten rid of it? Most likely, she assumed, so she asked about it. He said that he did throw it away, but she knew he was lying. When you're married, you are able to pick up on subtle hints. Reflexes that betray the body. For Clyde, it was his half-formed smile. So, she wondered what he could be lying about.

He had been sick after their fight. The past few

days he had started to look a little pale. His skin felt clammy, and the way he had been coughing, one would think he hacked out a lung. He constantly went to the kitchen to get a glass of water. He complained about getting chills, began dressing heavily around the house, and just felt tired as of late. She wanted to check if he was getting the flu. When your job involves going to a school filled with germ-carrying kids, a healthy man can easily get sick. However, being the stubborn man that he was, he insisted that he was just a little cold and it would pass on its own.

The last thing that concerned her was how they would be sitting in the living room watching television, and suddenly he would just get up. He would say that he had to use the bathroom or lie down, but he always had a distressed look as he left. It was one of the few times that he seemed to have any energy at all. She wondered if it had something to do with the fight they had, but when she tried to talk about it, he would shoot her down. And if she pressed on too much, it would cause another fight.

With Clyde, she found that it was best to not press on issues and let him open up when he was ready. She understood her husband wasn't ready to move on and that was understandable. What they both went through was the hardest thing they could ever experience. It was normal that they wouldn't easily move on. But she was concerned that if they didn't try to move on, they would be this way for the rest of her life. So, she continued giving lessons to Jacob and tried to act cheerful despite it all.

She had just finished the day at the bank and was on the road to her house. Their house was the second to last house in the suburb. The road was covered in snow, so she had to take her time driving. All the bright lights bouncing off the snow hurt her eyes and made her approaching home all the more desirable.

She parked her car and stepped out into the snow. She began walking to her porch, each of her footsteps accompanied by the sound of crunching snow. She stepped onto the first step of stairs to her porch.

"Maria!" someone called out for her. She turned and saw Rachel walking up towards her. She was surprised to be greeted by Rachel after what had happened with Jacob. Their last talk was about how her son wouldn't have any more piano lessons for a while. She stressed that she wasn't mad or harbored any negative feelings about what had happened, but just felt it would be better for her and Clyde if Jacob stopped coming by.

"Rachel, how are you doing?" she said, leaving the porch and walking to her.

"Oh, you know. Having to worry about all this snow and finding a babysitter for Jacob," she laughed. "How are you doing?"

"Oh, I'm fine. Just wanting to get inside and warm up."

"I know what you mean. So, uh, how has Clyde been lately? Nothing...strange has been going on, has it?"

"He's doing just fine, dealing with a cold, but fine. Thank you for asking?"

"Oh, I see." There was something about how she said it that struck Maria as odd.

"Is something wrong?" she offered.

"Well, it's just... I'm not really sure how to

explain it," Rachel said. "Well, you know how I like to walk my dog Rex around 9."

"Right." She was quite familiar with her routine. Rex was an overly excited German Shepherd that liked to jump on anyone he knew. He even knocked her down to the ground once to lick her face.

"Well, you see, I was walking him. He was particularly rowdy this morning and wanted to go to your house. While I tried to get a hold of him, I slipped and let go of the leash."

"Oh, that is never good," Maria joked.

"Yes. Rex ran behind your house and started barking. It wasn't playful either, it sounded like he was ready to attack."

"Really? That doesn't sound like Rex." Rex was excitable, but he never so much as growled at them or looked at them menacingly.

"So, I hurried to the back and got hold of the leash. Suddenly, the window opened and Clyde was looking at us," she said. "I'm not completely sure, but I think the window was in little Mary's room."

"What?" Maria said. "That's can't be. It had to be the other back window."

"That's what I thought, too, but when I think back to it...the wall behind him was pink." Only Mary's room had pink wallpaper. The rest of the house was a light blue.

"Are you sure?" Maria asked, wondering why he would be in her room. They both had stayed out since that day.

"I'm certain of it," Rachel said. "But that's not the part that worried me."

"What was?" she asked, feeling very anxious now.

"Well, you see, I waved and apologized, but he was mad. Shouted at me to—and I quote— 'Get that damn dog out of here.'" she said, doing air quotes as she did.

"No, there's no way he would have said that." Clyde always liked Rachel and thought the world of her. She had done a lot for them when they first moved into the neighborhood. It was hard to believe he would do that, but the hurt look on her face said it was true.

"But that's not all." Rachel said. "He said something that, well, struck me as odd."

"What was it?"

"Well, he screamed that '*the barking is making her cry*' before closing the window."

"Her?" Maria said, confused. "What do you mean her?" She thought about how he had been acting strange. About that day when they had that fight, how he mentioned crying. "What 'her' could he be talking about?"

"I don't know. I did notice that he was rather pale, but I guess that's just the cold," she said. Maria stood there, deep in thought. She turned to the house and wondered if he was going in Mary's room at night? When he would get up and had a distressed look on his face? Was he in there now? Did he still hear the crying?

"I…I see."

"You know me, I don't like to intervene in other people's lives, but I was just concerned about him. Is it possible that he may be coming down with something? That would explain why he was short with Jacob," she said. Maria began thinking the exact same thing. She wondered if a fever could make someone disoriented and hear things. She needed to go talk to him about this.

"Thank you, Rachel. I will make sure everything is okay. Don't you worry about it," she said with a forced smile.

"Just take care, okay? You two have been through so much already." Yes, they had. She walked away from Maria and headed back to her house. Once she was on her porch, she waved her goodbye and Maria did the same. Maria walked back onto the porch and noticed a note hanging off the screen door. She pulled it out of the grip of the door and read:

Hey Maria, I'm going to get us something to eat so don't make anything. Love you hon. -Clyde, 3:15 p.m.

She was worried about him going out in his condition, but there was nothing she could do about it now. She just had to hope that he would be okay. She entered the house and decided to play the piano. She walked down the hallway to the living room. She stopped and looked at the door of Mary's room and wondered why he had been going in there. She reached for the handle, but stopped before grabbing it. She looked at the picture of her sweet baby hanging from it, and her eyes began to tear up.

She wiped them away and walked to the living room. She thought that she had been ready to move on from what happened. Looking at the picture again confirmed that she wasn't. As she sat down behind the piano, she jerked her head to the hallway. For a moment, she thought she had heard something.

Maria was getting tired of playing Chopin as her husband came into the house. It was four now, and she wondered why getting takeout was taking so long. She had been scared that he might have crashed his car.

She got up from the piano and greeted him at the door.

"What took you so long?" she snapped.

"I'm sorry babe," he said, carrying Chinese take-out. "I went to the store to pick up some things." He sounded tired and his voice was coarse.

"You shouldn't be going out when you're sick." she scolded.

"I'm fine. In fact, I'm better than okay," he said, but without a hint of sarcasm. It sounded like he really believed it. He handed her the bag. "Take this to the kitchen for me. I'm going to get the rest."

"Well, let me help t-"

"NO!" He snapped back, stunning her. He must have seen it in her eyes. "That's okay, it's only a couple of bags." His voice was calmer now and he smiled. She could tell by his smile that he was lying, but took the take-out to the kitchen. "Thanks, and just go ahead and eat. You must be hungry."

"Okay." She listened in on him as he walked down the hallway. She heard him opening the door and assumed it was Mary's room. She wondered what he could be doing in the room. She knew that she had to talk to him.

About 10 minutes later, he walked into the kitchen. Maria hadn't eaten much of her food yet, as she was waiting for him. Although he was still sick, he had the air of happiness about him. She watched him get his plate ready with food.

"How are you doing?" she asked.

"I'm doing great. How was your day at work?" His tone sounded full of energy, but his sluggish movement told a different story. He sat his food at the table and took his seat. He looked at her, waiting for the answer to his question. She figured this was a good segue to their talk.

"Oh, not much happened. When I got home, Rachel came by to say hi."

"She did, huh?"

"Yes, she told me that she saw you in Mary's room." She decided to be upfront about this. "So… were you?"

"No, I don't believe I was," he rebutted. "I remember seeing her when I was in the restroom. Her dog was barking up a storm."

"She said that you shouted at her to get out. You wouldn't do that, would you?" She gave him a confrontational look.

"Yes, I did." He rubbed the back of his head. "I felt awful about that. I just woke up and the dog scared me you know. I hope she wasn't too mad." He smiled that self-betraying smile.

"She didn't seem too concerned about it."

"Oh, that's good," he said, stuffing his face with chicken and rice.

"Listen." She grabbed his hand and put it on the table. "I know things haven't been easy for us."

"Look, if this is about that fight we had…" He pulled his hand away from her. "I didn't mean it. I know you aren't replacing Mary. I shouldn't have said it."

"I know you didn't mean it, but you know you can talk to me whenever things become too much for you." He smiled a genuine smile and took her hand in his and looked her in the eyes.

"I know, honey. But I promise, everything is oka-" He stopped, his face morphing to distress and looked toward the hallway.

"Clyde? Are you okay?"

"I'm sorry, but I have to go." He said it like a man who realized he left the door to his house unlocked, nervous but trying to hide it. He lifted himself up from the chair, but before he could walk away, Maria grabbed his arm.

"What is it?" she asked, looking into his eyes. Had it been a week before his sudden illness, he could have pulled himself out of her grip, but now she was the stronger of the two.

"Honey, please, it's nothing." His half smile told her it wasn't. He tried to pull away, but she didn't loosen her grip.

"Clyde, tell me what's wrong!" she demanded.

"Seriously, there is nothing wrong. I just have to go to the bathroom." He had become increasingly panicked as he tried to free himself from her grasp.

"Stop lying!" she shouted. "What were you doing in Mary's room? Rachel said you said the dog was upsetting her. Who were you talking about?"

"LET GO NOW!" he shouted and slapped his free hand across her face. Her grip was broken and she staggered back. The swipe itself didn't hurt—Clyde was too weak to really have that effect—but it was the shock that caused her to let go. They were married for over four years and not once had he ever hit her before. He never even did anything to suggest it.

Clyde jolted to the hallway like he was trying to escape a burning building. Maria just stood there, still in shock of what had happened. She heard a door slam shut, which she assumed was Mary's room. She lowered herself to the floor and took a deep breath.

Had she made things worse now? Would he open up to her at all now? Would he be this aggressive when he recovered? What was going on? All of these questions swirled around in her mind like a whirlpool. She didn't realize the tears running down her cheeks until they dropped to the floor.

BBBBBBBBUUUUUUUUUZZZZZZZZZZ ZZZZZZZZZZZZZZZZZZZZZZZ

She heard something as she wiped away her tears. She wasn't sure what it was, but it sounded like a humming. It was similar to a bee, but much higher than that. She lifted herself up from the floor, wondering where it was coming from. She walked quietly into the hallway, thinking that she could hear it better there, but it was just as loud in the hallway as it was in the kitchen.

BBBBBBBBBBBBBBBBBUUUUUUUUUUZ ZZZZZZZZZZZZZZZZZZ

Maria felt slightly dizzy as she made her way through the hallway. There was something drawing her to it, trying to get her to find the source. She walked past Mary's room.

BBBBBBBBBBBBUUUUUUUU-
WAAAAAAAAAAAAAAAAAHHHHHHHHH

She stopped in her tracks when she heard it. That buzzing noise morphed into crying. And not just any cry. It was Mary. She felt her heart. Her dizziness had become more powerful, and she felt like she was going to lose her balance. She wondered if this was what Clyde was talking about all those days ago. Was this the reason for his behavior?

She leaned against the door and heard something under the crying. She placed her ear against the door to hear what was inside. It was faint, but she could tell it was her husband.

"There, there, it's alright now." She wondered who it was he was talking to. She remembered what Rachel told her about what happened in the morning.

She thought about what he said about hearing Mary crying. A thought came to her mind, one she wasn't sure was happy or scary: Was Mary in there now?

Could Mary be in the room, crying for her mommy and daddy? Maybe she would go in and see Clyde soothing her. She couldn't help but smile at the thought of her daughter being there. The thought that they could be a family again was like heaven to her. But why was she only just hearing her now? And what was that buzzing noise that turned into Mary's crying? She knew that something was very wrong.

"No, she's dead." Her eyes were filled with tears now. No matter how much she wanted it to be true, the crying from the room wasn't her daughter. She thought of things the crying could be from. Maybe Clyde had a recorder that played a baby crying and he was soothing Mary's old baby doll. Maybe he wanted to believe that Mary was still alive. But she knew better than that. She also knew she had to help her husband move on, too.

"Clyde!" She shouted over the crying and knocked at the door. "Are you in there?" She grabbed the doorknob and tried to turn it, but found it was locked. "Clyde, let me in?" She tried to turn the knob rapidly with vague hope that she could force it open.

"Everything is going to be okay," he said in a fatherly tone. She wasn't sure if he was even paying attention anymore. She started banging at the door and shouting his name. The crying continued to roar, but her focus was now on the door. She had to get into the room, get her husband's attention. She needed her husband back from whatever it was that was taking him away from her.

WAAAAAAAAHHHH-
BBBBBBUUUUUZZZZZZZZZZZZZZZ

She started slamming her body against the door. A loud boom followed each of her tackles against the wooden door. She felt a jolt of pain with each slam, but it did not stop her. She could still hear Clyde comforting whatever was in the room. She was determined to get him through this.

WAAAAAAAAAAAAHHHHHHHHHH-BUUUUZZZZZZZZZZZZ

The sound of crying had reverted back into the buzzing noise. What this meant she wasn't sure, but was not concerned with it. She backed away from the door for another tackle and took a deep breathe.

"AHHH!" She grunted as she slammed her body against the door once more, this time successfully forcing it open. Her shoulder pulsed in pain from hitting the door, but she was finally in. But when she saw her husband, she was truly terrified.

"There, there, it's all better now," Clyde said, rocking back and forth in the rocking chair. She didn't know what he was holding in his arms. It was like nothing she had ever seen before: the coarse fur, its limbs with claws, the lack of a mouth, but with small holes that seem to be the source of the buzzing. Its insect eyes had a faint red glow to them, the tail-like bottom with a needle at the end of it, the very needle that was injected into the nape of Clyde's neck. She stood there in horror as the tail seemingly pumped something from his neck. Just what was the hideous thing that had a hold on her husband?! Clyde sat there with the warm smile of a father at the disgusting thing that he held in his arm.

She realized that it was the same look he had when he would rock Mary to sleep. Did he see Mary in that thing? The thing feeding off of him?

The thought of Clyde believing that thing was Mary felt like blasphemy to the memories of their daughter. She would not allow it to take advantage of her grieving husband anymore. She grabbed the tail, its fur like that of a spider leg, prickly and revolting. She tried to pull it out, but the first try proved difficult. It would be the third attempt that she succeeded. Blood oozed out of the hole on the back of his neck. The tail tried to wiggle free of her grip. As it broke free of her grip, it shot from its needle end. It landed on Clyde's wound and began to sizzle.

"Maria, what are you doing?" The way he asked suggested he was in some sort of trance as it fed on him. "I'm taking care of Mar-" Before he could finish her name, she knocked the alien thing out of his arms. It hit the floor with a loud thump. The buzzing noise became louder and more intense than before. It began to wiggle, its limbs waving in the air as if it didn't know how to get up. Its tail hit the floor below it. "MARY!" He began to reach for the thing he thought was Mary, but Maria grabbed him by the arm.

"THAT'S NOT MARY!" She screamed and pulled him away. He thrashed and struggled against her, but he was much weaker now. Could that thing have done this to him? The image of that thing's tail in his neck was fresh in her mind, probably burnt into it for the rest of her life. She needed to get him away from it. She shut the door behind them as that high pitch buzz still rang so very loud.

Little over 20 minutes had passed since they left the room, and the high pitch buzz had not resigned. Clyde begged her to let him go back to Mary. But she refused to yield, despite his manic claims of her "being a bitch." It seemed the buzzing she heard was Mary's cries to him, so she didn't let it get to her. She was certain that he was under that thing's trace. Clyde tried to hit her, but it was all but useless at this point. It was like that creature was draining him of his energy and strength along with the blood.

Maria forced Clyde to stay seated on the couch in the living room as she thought of what to do. She felt anxious and restless as she paced back and forth in the living room, sometimes bumping against her piano. She wasn't sure what to do about that thing. What could she tell others about it? Would they even believe her? She doubted it, but she supposed she could show it to them. She looked outside and saw it was already dark. That was the winter evening for you, nighttime around five p.m.

If she wanted to show others the thing in Mary's room, she would have to leave the house. But what if it left while they were gone? She couldn't trust Clyde to keep an eye on it. She looked at her husband and was shocked by how pale he was now. He had the look of a wounded mother bear scared for its cub. Scared, angry, but not strong enough to do anything about it.

"Maria, please, I have to go to Mary!" he begged as she walked behind him. She placed her hand on his neck. She was shocked to see no hole there; there was only skin now. She was certain she saw the hole in the back of his neck, but she recalled that liquid shot out of the tail. She remembered how it sizzled. Did it heal his wound so there wouldn't be any trace of blood that could cause alarm? "Please let me go to her!" This brought her attention back. She needed to know what had happened over the past week.

She got in front of her husband and got on a knee, her hands on his arms to keep him from getting up, the way a mother would do when she had something important to tell her child. She studied his eyes, filled with desperation and fear.

"Clyde, what have you been doing this whole week?" she asked. "Were you going into Mary's room this whole time?" She already knew the answer to this, but felt she needed to take things one step at a time.

"Maria, I need to go-" he began to say.

"Just tell me and I will let you go to her." A promise she had no intention to keep, but she needed him to talk.

"It was a week ago," he said with no hesitation. "She was crying for me to calm her down."

"So, when did you go to Mary's room?" she asked.

"The night I heard the crying."

"So, what happened?"

"I saw her in her crib and I took care of her," he answered calmly. But his expression turned to anger. "She was crying, but I was the only one who heard her because I didn't forget about her! That's why you couldn't hear her!"

"What?" Is that what he thought? That because he wouldn't move on, he was being *rewarded* for it? Not a day went by that she hadn't thought about her toothless grin. Her husband's accusation sparked a small flame of anger in her that began to boil her blood. She slapped him across the face, just strong enough to knock him out of his chair.

"YOU THINK I WOULD EVER FORGET MY OWN DAUGHTER!?" She stood over him. Forgetting the baby that she carried for nine months, the baby that woke her up at night with her crying, the baby that filled her life with joy. Suggesting that felt like a knife through her heart and she would not hear it from her husband. "I will never forget the best part of my life. I can't." Tears began to flow down her cheeks as she began to cool down.

BBBBBBBUUUUUUUUUUUZZZZZZZZZ - WWAAAAAAAAAAAAAAHH

The buzzing had now turned back into crying and it was more powerful than before. Even though she knew it wasn't real, her instincts fought against her logic to go to the crying.

"WELL WHY COULDN'T YOU HEAR HER?!" Clyde shouted amidst the crying. He struggled to pick himself up after saying that. "You look at me like I'm crazy! Why is it that only I could hear her?" He threw his arms outward, his face covered in anger and resentment toward her.

"I don't know." It was a good question. She thought back to when she started hearing the crying. It was when she wasn't able to enter Mary's room and when he hit her. Why was it then she could hear it? What changed in her to hear the buzzing and crying? She thought back to her husband just a week ago and realized something. Although now he was very pale and sick, there wasn't that much of a change. Since Mary died, he was a man in deep grieving. So was she, but she tried to move on. He didn't.

"Now let me go to her!" he shouted. "You can't stop me anymore!" Maria knew she couldn't let him do that. She thought about the thing in Mary's room. That thing was a leech that was sucking the life out of her husband and would continue to do so until she stopped it. She knew what she had to do and without hesitation, she walked out of the living room. "Maria? Where are you going?"

She did not answer and instead walked into the kitchen. She opened the drawers on the counters, looking for it.

WWWAAAAAAAAAAAH-
BUUUUUUZZZZZZZZZZZZZZ

The buzzing had returned, this time even louder than before. Was this a sign that its illusion wasn't working on her anymore? She grew more resolved by it.

"Maria, what are you doing?" Clyde asked, holding to the wall to keep himself balance.

"I'm sorry, Clyde, but we need to move on." She found what she was looking for out. A knife for chopping vegetables. It wasn't their biggest, but it would work just as well. If her husband was to survive this, he needed to move on with his life, and in order to do that, she would have to kill the thing preventing him.

"Maria, no!" He said as soon as he realized her intention and tried to block the door. Maria didn't speak and tried to push him out of the way. But he wouldn't budge easily and grabbed her by the arm. "I said no!"

"Clyde, WE HAVE TO DO THIS!" She tried to pull back from him. She was surprised by this sudden strength he had. Perhaps his parental instincts were kicking in. She tried to pull away, but he grabbed the knife by the blade.

"AAAAWWWW!" He let out in pain as he pried it away from her. He shoved her onto the kitchen floor. He pointed the knife at her, both it and the palm of his hand covered in blood.

"Clyde, please listen," she pleaded.

"NO! I won't let you hurt her," he said with a crazy stare. Her heart was in her throat as she looked at him. She tried to crawl away from him and he took a step forward. She backed into the wall behind her. He grabbed her by the collar of her shirt and lifted her up.

"Please, Clyde. That thing is messing with your mind," she cried. "It's not Mary!!"

"YES. SHE. IS." He jabbed the knife into her stomach. A sharp pain shot through her as she hit the floor. She wasn't sure if this was really happening and looked at the wound. Her purple shirt was now growing a wet red spot with a tear in it. She placed her hand on the wound in part to see if she was imagining things. Her fears were confirmed.

She looked at her husband, standing there with fear, sorrow, and disgust in his eyes, perhaps directed towards himself. But above all else, there was determination. The determination to do anything to protect his *daughter*.

"Clyde," she whimpered, reaching up toward him.

"It didn't have to be like this." His voice cracked with regret and despair. "I wish you could have heard her, too."

"I did hear her today." Tears began to fill her eyes and her wound pounded. She shook her head mournfully. "But Mary is dead. She's not coming back." Since Mary died, it was a constant realization. Each time she passed her room, she thought of Mary. When she saw her bottle, saw mothers putting their baby strollers, saw children at play, she remembered Mary was never coming back.

"BUT SHE IS HERE." He shouted and raised the knife above his head. She laid there, preparing herself for the final strike. She saw tears running down Clyde's face as he hesitated.

BBBBBBUUUUUUUUUUUUUUUZZZZZ-WAAAAAAAAAAAAAAAAAAHHHHHH

That noise was still as clear and loud as it started. It was maddening to Maria. She realized that this would be the last sound she ever heard.

BANG!

A loud noise echoed through the house which caused Clyde to drop the knife. Maria's heart skipped a beat. It sounded like a door flinging open and hitting the wall. The high pitch buzzing had finally stopped, but Maria felt more concerned by it absence.

THUMP!
THUMP!
THUMP!

They could hear footsteps in the hallway and it got louder, as if it was coming closer.

"Clyde." Maria's voice had become shaken.

"I just remembered something," Clyde said. "When I went to Mary room that night…"

"What?"

"Before looking into the crib, I looked out the window."

"What happened?" she asked.

"I don't know, but I remember a bright light," he said in a nervous tone. Maria laid there and the thumping got closer. That was when something came to her about that creature in Mary's room…

There was something about that noise that was different from before. Its intensity and the way it wobbled. She thought about when Mary cried and how powerful it felt. The way it compelled her to hurry to her side. A baby's cries have a way of drawing its parents in to protect it.

Clyde still felt a little sick, but much better than before as he woke up in bed. Maria woke up and smiled at him, and he returned the gesture. She must have caught what he had because she had lost some of her color.

"Good morning," Maria said.

"Good morning, beautiful," he replied.

"So, are you going to get ready for school?" she asked. The snow had melted enough for there to be school, but he didn't feel like going today.

"Nah, I'm going to call off today. Maybe even tomorrow, too." He smiled. "You should do the same."

"I think I will," she said. "It's been awhile since I got a day off." She raised out of bed and rubbed the sleep from her eyes. Clyde looked out the window and saw the sun shining bright, the icicles hanging from the gutters dripping drops of water on the snow, creating a small, deep hole in it.

"Ow!" Maria cried.

"Are you okay?" Clyde turned to her. She was clutching at her bare stomach.

"I don't know why, but I just feel sore here." Her stomach looked fine to him.

"Maybe you ate something."

"Yeah, probably."

WWWWWWWWAAAAAAAAAAAAAAAA AAAHHHHHHHHHHHHHHHHH

Both of them turned their head to the door. It seemed like someone had woken up early.

"I will go calm her down," Maria said and began walking to the hallway.

"Wait, I will join you," Clyde said as he caught

up to her. They walked down the hallway and Maria opened the door.

"Hey there sweetie! Are you up early today?" She stepped into Mary's room with Clyde following her. They went to their daughter's crib and saw Mary was wide awake. When she saw them, she gave them her famous toothless grin.

"Aw, hey there," Clyde said as Maria lifted her out of the crib. She walked to the rocking chair. Clyde went to get a bottle for her. Once he handed it to Maria, she began feeding Mary. Mary looked at both of them with her pretty blue eyes as she sucked on the bottle. They both smiled as they looked at her lovingly.

"You know something, Maria?" Clyde said. "I just can't help but feel like the luckiest man on Earth."

"Me too," Maria said. "Me too."

That morning Clyde had a rather strange dream. He dreamt that he was a bird, flying to his nest. The bird flying next to him was Maria. They both flew to their nest with an egg in it.

When they landed on the tree, the egg began to shake. He and Maria circled the nest, looking at the egg. A crack formed in the shell and it got bigger until it fell apart. A chick poked its head out of the crack and began chirping. It was hungry and wanted to be fed.

Clyde was confused because the chick did not look familiar to him. But it was chirping at them and in their nest.

What else could it be?

Clyde and Maria took flight to look for food. As Clyde took off, he noticed another bird hanging from a different limb. It was a cuckoo bird.

But he couldn't worry about that because his

chick needed something to eat.

ABOUT THE AUTHOR

Ryne Green is an author living in Paintsville, KY. In addition to writing, he spends his days gaming and spending time with his niece Natalie and his beloved dog Cooper.

www.ingramcontent.com/pod-product-compliance
Lightning Source LLC
Chambersburg PA
CBHW030523130626
46549CB00007B/3081